THE MYSTERIOUS BOTTLE

A Children's Television Play

by

Debbie Nagioff & Peter Vincent

TSL Drama

irst published in Great Britain in 2023
By TSL Publications, Rickmansworth

ISBN: 978-1-915660-58-9

Cover by: Debbie Nagioff

CAST

(in order of appearance)

ETHAN	Aged 12
BETH	Aged 14
AUNT CHARLOTTE	Late 40s
UNCLE MALCOLM	Late 40s
PARROTT (DON BRADMAN)	Australian
COTTESLOE STAGE HANDS	
NICK SAVAGE (Theatre Director)	Mid 40s
BOY IN PLAYGROUND	Aged 13
TIMMS	Aged 15
MR PRODGER (Teacher)	Early 40s
PUPILS 1, 2 & 3	Aged 12 (all boys)
MRS SUSLOV	
MRS FARLEIGH (teacher)	Scottish – 30s
MRS PATEL (teacher)	
EMMA (pupil in Mrs Patel's class)	
BOY (pupil in Economics)	
PASSING WOMAN	
NEWSREADER ON RADIO	
POLICEMAN IN CAR	
WOMAN IN STREET	
ZARA	Aged 14
ANGRY WEEKEND SAILOR	
MAN 1, 2 and 3	
WOMAN ON BOAT COMING UPSTREAM	
RIVER POLICE	
POLICE MAN TRYING TO ARREST CHILDREN	
EXTRAS	

SCENE 1. INT: OPEN BEDROOM WINDOW: EARLY MORNING – DAY

FROM **BETH**'S PERSPECTIVE LOOKING OUT OF HER LARGE OPEN BEDROOM WINDOW STRAIGHT ONTO A RUSTLING TREE FRAMED BY BLOOD RED SUN GLOWING THROUGH. FROM THE GROUND WE HEAR **ETHAN** CALLING IN A LOUD WHISPER.

> **ETHAN**
>
> Come on, Beth!

> **BETH**
>
> I can't!

> **ETHAN**
>
> Yes you can. It's easy.

BETH TENTATIVELY LOOKS BEHIND HER.

> **BETH**
>
> Shh!

> **ETHAN**
>
> Hurry up!

> **BETH**
>
> Okay!

SCENE 2. AUNT CHARLOTTE'S BEDROOM

CUT TO A SLEEPING **CHARLOTTE**.

SCENE 3. GARDEN SCENE: EXT: EARLY MORNING

FROM **ETHAN**'S POINT OF VIEW WE SEE **BETH** REACHING OUT TO GRAB THE NEAREST BRANCH.
CUT TO **ETHAN** AT BOTTOM OF TREE.

> **ETHAN**
>
> Got the money?

> **BETH**
>
> [*Nodding*] Yes of course I've got the money.

                                    ETHAN

Come on.

                                    BETH

I'm trying.

                                    ETHAN

Girls are rubbish!

                                    BETH

I'm not.

                                    ETHAN

Wish I'd had a brother.

BETH TAKES A LEAP OF FAITH AND GRABS THE TREE. SHE LETS OUT A GASP, RIPS HER DRESS.

SCENE 4.UNCLE MALCOLM'S BEDROOM: INT: EARLY MORNING

UNCLE **MALCOLM** IS SLEEPING. HIS **PARROT**, 'DON BRADMAN' IS SITTING ON ITS PERCH.

                              DON BRADMAN

[*Two Ronnies impression*] It's goodnight from me, and it's good night from him.

                                  MALCOLM

[*half asleep*] Shut up!

SCENE 5. STREET SCENE: EXT: EARLY MORNING

ETHAN EMERGING FROM A CORNER SHOP WITH AN *A TO Z*. **CHARLOTTE** COMES OUT BEHIND HIM.

                                    ETHAN

How much did you nick?

                                    BETH

Thirty quid.

                                    ETHAN

Right, the *A to Z* was three quid. We got 27 quid left now. Come on.

                              BETH

Is this gonna work?

                              ETHAN

Trust me.

SCENE 6. CHARLOTTE'S BEDROOM: INT: EARLY MORNING

AUNT **CHARLOTTE** IS JUST GETTING UP. SHE PUTS ON HER DRESSING GOWN AND PINK FLUFFY SLIPPERS

                            CHARLOTTE

Beth? Ethan? Time to get up. Malcolm, go and wake those bloody kids.

SCENE 7. AERIAL VIEW OF LONDON: EXT: DAY

PAN ACROSS SOUTH BANK. CLOSE UP OF NATIONAL THEATRE.

SCENE 8. CAFÉ AT NATIONAL THEATRE: INT: DAY

CLOSE UP OF **BETH** AND **ETHAN**. **ETHAN** IS EATING EGG AND CHIPS AND HAS A CHOCOLATE MILKSHAKE. **BETH** HAS A COFFEE AND A CROISSANT.

                              BETH

We shouldn't have wasted all that money. How much is left?

ETHAN PULLS OUT DIRTY HANKY, CHEWING GUM, A SCOOBIDOO, COINS AND A £10 NOTE. HE PUTS IT ALL ON THE TABLE.

                              BETH

Yuk! Put that snotty thing away.

                              ETHAN

You're snotty. We've got 15 quid.

                              BETH

Maybe I should keep it.

                              ETHAN

No. I'm looking after it.

                              BETH

Ethan, stop arguing. You're always arguing.

                              ETHAN
When are we going to see Nick?

                              BETH
I don't know if he'll see us.

                              ETHAN
Why?

                              BETH
Well...we might need an appointment.

                              ETHAN
An appointment? It's not the dentist!

CUT TO

SCENE 9. STAGE DOOR OF COTTESLOE: EXT: DAY

THE **CHILDREN** ARRIVE AT STAGE DOOR. IT'S OPEN. **STAGE HANDS** ARE GOING IN AND OUT. ARTIFICIAL FOLIAGE AND OTHER SCENERY IS BEING BROUGHT IN AND OUT.

                              ETHAN
    Let's go in.

                              BETH
What if someone stops us?

                              ETHAN
We'll say we're Rowena Daniels' children and we have an appointment with Nick Savage.

                              BETH
But we don't.

                              ETHAN
You are <u>well</u> annoying! Go 'ome if you want.

                              BETH
No. I'm staying.

                              ETHAN
Look, there ain't no security on the door. Piece of piss!

                              BETH
What do we do then?

WE SEE **ETHAN** LOOKING AT THE FOLIAGE HE WALKS TOWARDS IT AND PICKS UP A
FALSE TREE.

                              BETH
Eeth!

                              ETHAN
Come on then.

SCENE 10. COTTESLOE THEATRE: INT: DAY

STAGE HANDS ARE BUSYING ABOUT. **NICK** SAVAGE IS IN THE STALLS SLOUCHED
LOOKING AT A SCRIPT IN CONFERENCE WITH SOMEBODY NEXT TO HIM.

ENTER **BETH** TRYING TO HIDE BEHIND HER BROTHER WHO IS CARRYING A TREE. SHE
LOOKS AWKWARD. **NICK** SAVAGE LOOKS UP AS **ETHAN** PUTS THE TREE DOWN.

                              NICK
Is it me or are the stage hands getting younger?

                              ETHAN
Look that must be him.

                              BETH
Where?

                              ETHAN
In them chairs.

NICK PEERS CLOSELY AT THEM.

                              NICK
Can I help you?

                              ETHAN
Hi Nick.

                              BETH
Call him Mr Savage. Don't you remember, Mr Savage, Beth and Ethan.
Rowena's kids.

                              NICK
Rowena? And you're Beth. You look like her. You both do.

ETHAN

No, I'm a bloke.

NICK

[*laughs*]

Oh my God.

CUT AWAY TO

SCENE 11. CHARLOTTE'S DINING ROOM: INT: DAY

CLOSE UP OF **CHARLOTTE**, FROWNING. WE SEE THE **PARROT**, DON BRADMAN FLYING. **CHARLOTTE** IS STILL STARING AT THE PHONE AND THEN SLAMS IT DOWN.

CHARLOTTE

[*calling*] Malcolm? Malcolm?

PARROT FLIES AROUND HER HEAD. SHE PUSHES IT OFF.

CHARLOTTE

Bloody parrot.

DON BRADMAN

She's an old trout.

CHARLOTTE

He taught you that! Thank you, Malcolm! Malcolm, Malcolm, the children have run off again.

SCENE 12. COTTESLOE THEATRE: INT: DAY

NICK SAVAGE AND THE **CHILDREN** ARE SITTING IN THE STALLS TALKING.

NICK

I was very fond of your mum. She was a great actress and a wonderful singer.

BETH

She still is.

NICK

But she couldn't always hold things together.

                              BETH

How do you mean?

                              NICK

She'd not turn up on time for rehearsals. That annoyed people. The
actors and crew were always waiting for her. But I'm very fond of her,
as you know. I wish she could still be here. But if she's in rehab, I
can't interfere.

                              ETHAN

What's rehab?

                              BETH

We haven't heard from Mum since we went to Aunt Charlotte's.

                              NICK

Aunt Charlotte? [*pause*] Is she still chewing on a wasp?

                        BETH AND **ETHAN**

Yeah! [*laughter*]

                              BETH

But Mum ain't written to us or anything.

                              NICK

Look, ask her to contact me.

                              BETH

We'll try.

                              NICK

And I'll try to help. [*looking towards cast and crew*] With you in a
moment, guys.

                              BETH

We'd better go then.

                              NICK

You even speak like her.

BETH HUGS HIM. **ETHAN** IS ABOUT TO HUG HIM, BUT SHAKES HIS HAND INSTEAD.

SCENE 13. THE FOUNTAINS OUTSIDE THE BFI: EXT: DAY

LOTS OF RUNNING IN AND OUT OF THE FOUNTAINS. GETTING DRENCHED AND GIGGLING.

> BETH
>
> You're getting soaked.

> ETHAN
>
> So are you.

> BETH
>
> Oh, Eeth! Enough! Come on out. We're meant to be at school.

> ETHAN
>
> You are well boring. I ain't going.

FAST WIPE TO

SCENE 14. OUTSIDE NATIONAL FILM THEATRE: EXT: DAY

BETH LOOKING AT BOOKSTALL, EATING A HAMBURGER. ETHAN STARTS WALKING DOWN THE STEPS TOWARDS THE RIVER.

> BETH
>
> Don't go too far.

> ETHAN
>
> I'm only going down to that little beach.

> BETH
>
> You're not allowed.

> ETHAN
>
> Who said?

> BETH
>
> Just be careful.

> ETHAN
>
> Okay.

CLOSE UP OF BEACH AND RIVER, AND AN UNUSUAL BOTTLE FLOATING TOWARDS ETHAN DOWNSTREAM.

ETHAN

Wow, that's cool.

BETH

What is?

ETHAN PICKS UP UNUSUAL BOTTLE.

BETH

Ethan, put it down. It's dirty.

ETHAN

No it ain't. It's been washed by the river.

BETH

It's polluted. Chuck it.

ETHAN

Oy, stop telling me what to do. Hey, it's got funny writing on it.

BETH STANDS. **ETHAN** WALKS UP TOWARDS HER WITH THE BOTTLE.

ETHAN

That is sick!

BETH

Get rid of it.

ETHAN

Hang on, there's something inside. It's paper all rolled up.

BETH

Here, let me.

ETHAN

I'll do it. I found it.

BETH

You're such a baby.

HE STRUGGLES AND CAN'T RETRIEVE PAPER.

ETHAN

Have to break it then. Stand aside.

BETH

No Ethan. Somebody might see you.

ETHAN SMASHES THE BOTTLE AGAINST SIDE OF BANK, AND CUTS HIS THUMB.

ETHAN

Done it. Ouch! I've cut meself now.

ETHAN PULLS OUT THE MESSAGE BUT HIS THUMB IS BLEEDING.

BETH

Told you! Twit!

SHE PULLS OUT HER HANKY AND PROCEEDS TO WRAP IT ROUND **ETHAN**'S THUMB.
ETHAN TRIES TO READ NOTE.

BETH

That paper'll have germs on it.

ETHAN

Germs! You freak! Ah! I can't read this. It's all rubbish.

HE CHUCKS IT ON THE GROUND.

BETH

Don't chuck it! That's litter. Pick it up.

ETHAN

[*picking it up and handing it to* **BETH**] You said it had germs.

BETH

Wait. It's not like French or anything.

ETHAN

Could be a special spy code.

BETH

Don't be daft. Why would a spy stick a message in a bottle? That's
mad that is. Give it me.

ETHAN

No. It's mine. I found it. [*puts it in his pocket*]

BETH

Well, look after it then. Come on, let's go 'ome.

SCENE 15. THE FINSBURY PARK HOUSE: EXT: EARLY EVENING

FRONT OF **CHARLOTTE**'S HOUSE. THERE IS A FLICKER OF NET CURTAINS, DOWNSTAIRS WINDOW. THE CHILDREN WALK INTO SHOT AND COME UP GARDEN PATH. AUNT **CHARLOTTE** FLINGS OPEN FRONT DOOR.

> **CHARLOTTE**
>
> Where have you been? And where's my money? Get inside, this minute.

THE **CHILDREN** LOOK AT EACH OTHER GLUMLY, THEN GO IN THE FRONT DOOR.

SCENE 16. AUNT CHARLOTTE'S DINING TABLE: INT: EARLY EVENING

MALCOLM IS SITTING DOWN AT A TABLE SET FOR TWO, ONLY. **BETH** AND **ETHAN** HAVE BEEN MADE TO SIT AND WATCH. UNCLE **MALCOLM** LOOKS UNCOMFORTABLE. AUNT **CHARLOTTE** IS PACING UP AND DOWN ANGRILY.

> **CHARLOTTE**
>
> If I'd known that sister of mine had brought her children up to steal, I would never have taken you in.

> **BETH**
>
> We're very sorry, we did mean ...
>
> Didn't your mother teach you anything?

> **MALCOLM**
>
> They look cold dear.

> **CHARLOTTE**
>
> And you can shut up! There's no supper for either of you.

MALCOLM LOOKS AT THE **CHILDREN** SYMPATHETICALLY AND PULLS A CARTOON FACE, AS HE IS TOLD OFF. **CHARLOTTE** LEAPS UP AND STARTS CLEARING AWAY THE TABLE.

> **ETHAN**
>
> We're hungry.

> **BETH**
>
> Mum wouldn't like that.

CHARLOTTE

Your mum's not here. She doesn't give a damn about you. Go to your room. Give me your plate, Malcolm.

MALCOLM

I haven't finished, dear.

SHE WHIPS THE PLATE AWAY FROM HIM.

CHARLOTTE

You have now. Go to your room.

MALCOLM

Who me?

CHARLOTTE

Not you, you fool! Them! Go on, off you go. I don't want to see you till the morning.

THE **CHILDREN** GET UP AND LOOK AT **CHARLOTTE**. THEY LEAVE. **MALCOLM** MAKES A SUFFERING FACE AT THEM.

CUT TO

SCENE 17. BETH AND ETHAN'S BEDROOM

COLD AND SPARSE WITH A BARE LIGHT BULB, MAKESHIFT CURTAIN BETWEEN BEDS, TO MAKE THEM FEEL UNCOMFORTABLE AND ILL AT EASE. **BETH** IS SAYING HER PRAYERS.

BETH

I know I've said this before but I do want my mum. Not anyone else. Just my mum. Thank you God in anticipation. Amen. Oh and PS Ethan sends his love. He's a bit tired now and hungry again.

SHE GETS UP. ENTER **ETHAN** STUDYING THE PIECE OF PAPER.

BETH

Oh, throw that thing away.

ETHAN

No. I think this is a message for us.

BETH

Come off it. They didn't know we were going to be there!

ETHAN

They could have done if they were extra terrestitrals [*sic*]. They can see into our minds.

BETH

Let's look at it again.

ETHAN HANDS IT TO BETH. THERE'S A KNOCK AT THE DOOR. SHE QUICKLY HANDS IT BACK TO HIM.

BETH

Stash it. Quick!

ETHAN

[*Pitching*] Yeah?

IN WALKS **MALCOLM** WITH A TRAY OF DRINKS AND SOME PEANUT BUTTER SANDWICHES. THE **PARROT** IS ON HIS SHOULDER.

ETHAN

Malcolm!

MALCOLM

Shh!

ETHAN

Thanks, Unc.

BETH

Thank you. Thank you.

MALCOLM

Ssh, you'll wake her up.

DON BRADMAN

Hello, you two!

ALL THREE

Ssh!

SCENE 18. SCHOOL PLAYGROUND: EXT: DAY

ETHAN IS STANDING AROUND ON HIS OWN, KICKING STONES. BOISTEROUS **CROWD OF BOYS** ARE PLAYING FOOTBALL WITH A TENNIS BALL. THEY SEEM TO MOVE TOWARDS **ETHAN**.

BOY IN PLAYGROUND

[*to* **ETHAN**] Hey, get out the way, Daniels, you tosser...

ETHAN

Who are you calling a tosser?

ON THE OTHER SIDE OF THE GROUP, ALSO ON HIS OWN IS A BOY CALLED **TIMMS**, A SCHOLARLY, BESPECTACLED BOY PLAYING A HARMONICA. HE IS WALKING ALONG OBLIVIOUS TO EVERYONE ELSE.

BOY IN PLAYGROUND

Get out the way Timms, you specoid.

THEY COLLIDE WITH **TIMMS**, KNOCK HIM TO THE GROUND AND HIS GLASSES GET KNOCKED OFF HIS FACE. **TIMMS** STARTS TO FEEL AROUND FOR SPECTACLES AND HARMONICA.

BOY IN PLAYGROUND

What's the matter Timms? Lost something?

CUT TO **ETHAN** APPROACHING AND CONCERNED.

TIMMS

I can't find my specs.

BOY IN PLAYGROUND

What's that? You can't find your what?

TIMMS

My glasses.

BOY IN PLAYGROUND

[*picking up the specs*] Oh, you mean these?

TIMMS

Can I have them?

THE **BOYS** START TO LAUGH AND THE SPECS ARE THROWN AROUND FROM ONE BOY TO ANOTHER.

BOY IN PLAYGROUND
What's the magic word, Geek?

TIMMS
Sorry, <u>please</u> can I have my glasses. I can't see.

BOY IN PLAYGROUND
Hear that? He can't see.

BOYS ALL LAUGH. **ETHAN** APPROACHES.

ETHAN
Oy, you lot, give him his glasses.

BOY IN PLAYGROUND
Shut up. Shitface. Here you are 'speccy, spec, spec, spec'.

HE THROWS THE SPECS ON THE FLOOR IN FRONT OF **TIMMS**. **TIMMS** REACHES OUT FOR THEM, BUT THE **BOY** STAMPS ON THE GLASSES AND BREAKS THEM. **ETHAN** STARTS FIGHTING WITH THE **BOY**. THEN ALL THE **BOYS** START FIGHTING AND PUNCHING **ETHAN**. **TIMMS** CRAWLS OUT FROM UNDERNEATH. **BETH** SEES HER BROTHER FIGHTING.

BETH
Hey, leave him alone. Ethan.

WHISTLE BLOWN BY MR **PRODGER**, THE ON DUTY TEACHER.

MR PRODGER
Oy, you lot, stop that now. You'll be in trouble.

CHEERS FROM ALL THE **BOYS**. SCHOOL BELL RINGS IN FOUR LONG PROLONGED YET INTERMITTENT BUZZES.

MR PRODGER
Shut up the lot of you. [*under breath*] Little bastards. Saved by the bell. Get inside.

CHILDREN FILE PAST MR PRODGER. SOME OF THE **BOYS** GIVE HIM A V SIGN BEHIND HIS BACK. **ETHAN**'S FACE IS BLEEDING FROM THE FIGHT. HE APPROACHES **TIMMS**.

ETHAN

Are you okay, Timms?

TIMMS

Yeah, you?

ETHAN

Yeah.

TIMMS

Can't see without my glasses.

MR PRODGER

Oy, get inside you two.

OLD TENNIS BALL HITS MR **PRODGER** ON THE SIDE OF THE HEAD. HE REACTS.

SCENE 19. STALLS, COTTESLOE THEATRE: INT: DAY

NICK SAVAGE IS ON HIS MOBILE TO **ROWENA**'S AGENT.

NICK

Jack, Nick Savage here...I'm fine, and yourself?...Good, good. Listen, Jack, Rowena Daniels, are you still handling her?...Oh. Would you still have a phone number or address for her?...Oh I see. I'd heard she'd been ill...Rehab? Do you know where?...You don't. I'll try something else. Thanks Jack.

SCENE 20. MR PRODGER'S ENGLISH CLASS: INT: DAY

THE CLASS ARE STUDYING *PRIDE & PREJUDICE*. MR **PRODGER** IS DRONING ON IN THE BACKGROUND. ON THE WHITE BOARD IS A DIAGRAM WITH THE NAMES OF THE BENNETT SISTERS AND THEIR CHARACTER STUDIES. **ETHAN** IS SLOUCHED ON THE DESK DOODLING ON IT. AN EXERCISE BOOK IS OPEN.

MR PRODGER

Now, we've read how Lydia has eloped with Wickham. So can anybody tell me the significance of Mr Darcy's role in bringing about their marriage?

PUPIL 1

'Cause he felt like it, sir?

MR PRODGER

No. No. No. Someone else?

SEVERAL **PUPILS** PUT THEIR HANDS UP.

PUPIL 2

Because he was rich?

MR PRODGER

Well he did earn £10,000 a year, as you know. But not the answer I was looking for.

PUPIL 3

Sir, this is a rather girlie book. Can't we read something else?

CUT TO **ETHAN** WHO HAS PULLED OUT THE MYSTERIOUS MESSAGE AND IS TRYING TO DECIPHER IT.

MR PRODGER

No you can't. It's a set book. On the curriculum.

MR PRODGER

So, what do you think, Daniels?

ETHAN

Me?

MR PRODGER

Yes, you.

ETHAN IS READING THE NOTE UNDER DESK. MR **PRODGER** APPROACHES.

ETHAN

I...er...

MR PRODGER

What did I just say?

ETHAN

Erm.

MR PRODGER

Erm! What have you got under the desk?

  ETHAN

    It's private.

BOYS LAUGH.

                                    MR PRODGER

    Give it to me.

                                        ETHAN

    It's mine.

                                    MR PRODGER

Give it to me, <u>now</u>.

ETHAN HESITATES.

                                    MR PRODGER

    Come on, come on. I haven't got all day. [*he pulls it out of* **ETHAN**'s
    hand and it tears in half] Now, let's see. [*turns the pieces round,
    upside down etc.*] Looks to be Cyrillic.

                                        ETHAN

    Sir?

                                    MR PRODGER

    Russian, probably. Here you are. Now get back to your book.

ETHAN LOOKS AT THE TORN MESSAGE.

SCENE 21. EMPTY SCHOOL CLASSROOM AT LUNCHTIME: INT: DAY

ETHAN IS SHOWING TIMMS THE MESSAGE, WHICH HAS NOW BEEN CELLOTAPED BACK
TOGETHER.

                                        ETHAN

    He said it was Sillic or something.

                                        TIMMS

    Where did you get this?

                                        ETHAN

    From the river, up London. In a bottle.

                                        TIMMS

    I've seen writing like this on old newsreels of Russian rockets. They
    had this writing on the side.

ETHAN

Yeah? Can you read what it says?

TIMMS

I've got an idea.

ETHAN

What?

TIMMS

Take it to the Russian Embassy. They'll translate it for you.

ETHAN

Where's that? Moscow?

TIMMS

No, in London. I could come with you.

ETHAN HOLDS PAPER UP TO THE LIGHT. AS HE DOES SO, PUPIL 1 RACES PAST AND GRABS THE NOTE OUT OF HIS HAND

PUPIL 1

Yahoo!

ETHAN

Oy! Give that back.

PUPIL 1 STARTS TO RUN WITH IT, AND TEAR IT UP. ETHAN CHASES HIM, GRABS HIM AND PUSHES HIM TO THE FLOOR.

PUPIL 1

You're dead meat, you are.

ETHAN PICKS UP THE PIECES. PUPIL 1 RUNS OFF.

SCENE 22. CORNER SHOP: EXT: DAY

CLOSE UP OF SIGN SAYING 'PHOTOCOPYING - 10P PER SHEET'. MALCOLM IS STANDING OUTSIDE WITH 'DON BRADMAN' WHO IS SITTING ON HIS SHOULDER. ETHAN EMERGES WITH FIVE PHOTOCOPIES OF THE MESSAGE, WHICH HAS BEEN STUCK TOGETHER.

UNCLE MALCOLM

Alright?

                              ETHAN

Thanks Uncle for the dosh.

THEY START STROLLING OFF.

                             MALCOLM

That was a loan not a gift.

                              ETHAN

I know. I know.

                             MALCOLM

So, is it for a school project or something?

                              ETHAN

It's private.

                             MALCOLM

Oh <u>private</u> is it? It's something dubious isn't it?

                              ETHAN

What's dubious?

                             MALCOLM

This. All this.

                          DON BRADMAN

[*sings*] Fly me to the moon.

                             MALCOLM

That's enough.

SCENE 23. MALCOLM'S OFFICE: INT:EARLY EVENING

BETH QUIETLY ENTERS **MALCOLM**'S OFFICE AND STARTS LOOKING AROUND. INSIDE
OLD FASHIONED ROLL TOP BUREAU, VARIOUS CHAIRS, A VERY HIGH BOOK SHELF
ETC, AND PAPERWORK. SHE STARTS LOOKING AROUND VARIOUS DRAWERS AND COMES
TO THE DESK. **ETHAN** SUDDENLY JUMPS OUT FROM BEHIND A CURTAIN.

                              ETHAN

Boo!

                              BETH

[*Jumps*] Stop it!

                        ETHAN

Wonder what he keeps in there? [*indicating the bureau*]

                        BETH

I'm not sure we should look.

                        ETHAN

Typical. Stand back.

ETHAN STARTS TO FIDDLE AROUND WITH IT. INSIDE HE FINDS A MOBILE PHONE.

                        ETHAN

Wow. A Blackberry.

                        BETH

Put it back.

                        ETHAN

Let's phone Mum.

                        BETH

We don't know where she is.

                        ETHAN

I'm going to ring home anyway.

HE IS ABOUT TO CALL. ENTER **MALCOLM**.

                        MALCOLM

Hey, what are you two doing?

                      BETH/ETHAN

Nothing.

                        MALCOLM

I see. And what are you doing with my phone?

                        ETHAN

We want to ring Mum.

                        BETH

Can we, Uncle? Can we?

                        MALCOLM

Cost you a fiver.

                                        BETH
  We ain't got a fiver.

ENTER **CHARLOTTE**.

                                      CHARLOTTE
  What are you all doing in here?

                              BETH/ETHAN/MALCOLM
  Nothing.

SCENE 24. SCHOOL LIBRARY: INT: DAY

TIMMS AND **ETHAN** ARE WAITING TO USE A SCHOOL COMPUTER. ALL THE COMPUTERS
ARE OCCUPIED.

                                       TIMMS
  We're only allowed 15 minutes at a time.

BOY GETS UP FROM COMPUTER.

                                       TIMMS
  Oh thanks.

                                       ETHAN
  Ta.

TIMMS STARTS TO TYPE QUICKLY. **ETHAN** LOOKS OVER HIS SHOULDER.

                                       ETHAN
  What are you going to search?

CLOSE UP OF GOOGLE SCREEN.

                                       TIMMS
  Let's try Russian translators in this area.

WE SEE DETAILS OF A **DR SUSLOV**, WHO IS A WRITER AND TRANSLATOR OF ENGLISH
INTO RUSSIAN AND RUSSIAN INTO ENGLISH.

                                       TIMMS
  That might be our man.

                                       ETHAN
  Mr Suss-lev [*reading phonetically and slowly*]

                           TIMMS

   Get in there!

SCENE 25. STREET SCENE IN THE NORTH LONDON AREA: EXT: DAY

WE SEE **ETHAN** AND **TIMMS** APPROACHING A HOUSE ON A BUSY ROAD.

                           TIMMS

   This is it.

                           ETHAN

   Shall I knock?

                           TIMMS

   Well, you found the message.

                           ETHAN

   Okay.

HE KNOCKS. NO ANSWER AT FIRST. **TIMMS** GETS A HARMONICA OUT OF HIS POCKET
AND IS ABOUT TO PLAY IT.

                           ETHAN

   Nobody.

                           TIMMS

   Oh well. [*starts to play a tune*]

THE DOOR IS OPENED BY AN **ELDERLY LADY.**

                         MRS SUSLOV

   Yes?

                           TIMMS

   Oh, sorry. [*pockets the harmonica*]

                         MRS SUSLOV

   Can I help you?

                           TIMMS

   Go on. Ask her.

                           ETHAN

   Mr Susslev please?

MRS SUSLOV

It's Suslov. I'm afraid you're too late. My husband died six months ago.

ETHAN

Oh sh (it).

TIMMS

[*interrupting*] We're sorry to bother you. Let's go, Ethan.

MRS SUSLOV

Wait a minute. I'm <u>Mrs</u> Suslov. Can I help?

ETHAN

Well I found a note, well a piece of paper. [*he shows it to her*] I thought he could help us with it.

MRS SUSLOV LIFTS HER HAND AS IF TO ASK HIM TO WAIT. SHE READS THE NOTE.

MRS SUSLOV

Where did you get this?

ETHAN

We found it, in a bottle.

MRS SUSLOV

In a bottle? [*short laugh*] I read Mr Edgar Allen Poe, too. All right. Come back tomorrow at 5.00 p.m. and I'll see what I can do.

ETHAN/TIMMS

[*ad lib*] Oh thank you Mrs Suslov. Thank you.

MRS SUSLOV

You are welcome. Now be careful on the path. It's all in a bit of a mess since –

TIMMS

Goodbye.

THE **BOYS** ARE EXCITED. THEY LEAVE.

SCENE 26. STALLS. COTTESLOE THEATRE: INT: DAY

NICK SAVAGE IS TAKING A BREAK. HIS MOBILE PHONE STARTS TO RING. ITS RING TONE IS MOZART'S 'THE MAGIC FLUTE' HE ANSWERS IT.

NICK

Hello. [*pause*] Hello?

THERE IS A CLICK ON THE OTHER END. HE CHECKS THE PHONE NUMBER.

NICK

Rowena!

SCENE 27. MRS SUSLOV'S FRONT LOUNGE: INT: EARLY EVENING

THE **BOYS** ARE SITTING EATING TEA. **TIMMS** IS MAKING NOTES AS **MRS SUSLOV** TRANSLATES THE NOTE.

MRS SUSLOV

The girl, she say her name is Zara. She says she can <u>hear</u> cows.

TIMMS

<u>Hear</u> cows. Can't she see them?

MRS SUSLOV

I don't know. It seems she sees <u>nothing</u>.

ETHAN

Maybe she's blindfolded.

TIMMS

Yes.

MRS SUSLOV

It is possible. *Ya nes nayow!* I don't know. She say she hear children, noise from factory siren and fireworks. Fancy! This note is very interesting. Where did you find it, again?

ETHAN

[*pause*] In a bottle.

TIMMS

On the Thames.

TIMMS

Sounds like she's a prisoner.

MRS SUSLOV

At least she's not in Siberia. Just a little Russian joke.

ETHAN

What?

MRS SUSLOV

[*short laugh*] Do not be depressed, child. And now I am tired. So you must go and have a nice life.

TIMMS AND **ETHAN** LOOK AT EACH OTHER. THEY GET UP AND LEAVE.

SCENE 28. MRS FARLEIGH'S CLASSROOM: INT: DAY

BETH IS IN THE CLASSROOM ON HER OWN WITH MRS **FARLEIGH**. MRS **FARLEIGH** UNROLLS A HUGE MAP AND PUTS IT ON A DESK.

MRS FARLEIGH

Well, Beth, I admire your enthusiasm, but as you can see the Thames covers quite an area. Look at this. It's the longest river in England.

BETH

It would be.

MRS FARLEIGH

What was it you were looking for?

BETH

Somewhere there's boats.

MRS FARLEIGH

Boats? Boats are everywhere. Look at the course of the river. It doesn't just go through London. It flows through Oxford and down to London. And look, there's Reading over here. Oh and there's Richmond and Windsor.

BETH

Can I borrow the map for a few days?

ROLLING THE MAP UP VERY QUICKLY.

MRS FARLEIGH

Oh, no, no, no. I can't do that. School property.

BETH

But, what am I going to do?

MRS FARLEIGH

[Concerned] Beth, is everything all right at home?

BETH

I dunno Miss. I don't live at home.

SCENE 29. BETH AND ETHAN'S BEDROOM: INT:EARLY EVENING

ETHAN HAS A BLACK EYE and BRUISES, AND IS SITTING ON HIS BED. ENTER BETH, OUT OF SORTS, DUMPS HER SCHOOL BAG.

BETH

Oh bloody Norah! Now what?

ETHAN

Just cos I give that one a dead leg. There was seven of them.

BETH

Had time to count, did you? Better get you to Auntie C...

ETHAN

No! No. I'm all right.

BETH

Mmm. I've only got some of that stuff that stings...

ETHAN

I won't scream or nothing. Like in that film.

BETH

Oh, shut up...You ask for trouble, you do. Oh sugar...Can't find it.

ETHAN

Don't worry. I'll be all right.

BETH:

Stop being...Stop being a bloody hero...Why don't people shut <u>up</u>?

DUMPS HERSELF AT END OF BED, SOBS BRIEFLY.

ETHAN

What? wha's the matter?

BETH

You don't know. Most the girls in my class have, well, make-up, eyeliner and that, hair extensions...They look great. Oh, you wouldn't understand. Mum's never wrote to us. She don't care. We feed that bloody bird. Not a word of thanks. I've had enough, Eeth. Up to here. We could - we could just do a runner, couldn't we? South America's nice. Brazil! Second largest exporter of soya beans. We done that today.

ETHAN

[*getting himself up into sitting position*] You what? You're mad. What about the girl? What about our thing - our mission? That bottle was sent to <u>me</u>. For me to pick up. Me, right? Well, and you in a way.

BETH

Oh, it's all a game. Colonel Mustard in the billiards room with the lead piping...I can't be doin' with it. And that's-

ETHAN

Beth! We said...And we'll do it. Save that girl, Zara, right? There could be a reward.

BETH

I don't think there is a reward. Or even a Zara.

ETHAN

Might be one. And then we'll go to South America. Rio! The three of us! They've got statues there of God and that and funny processions and beaches. You can live on a beach.

BETH

Eeth, you're so...sort of...sort of nerdy. We're not gonna find no girl. Not ever. See? Look. The River Thames, right? It's 200 bleedin' miles long. And I reckon that bloody letter's a con or April fool - Just waiting for a dork like you.

A KNOCK AT THEIR DOOR.

BETH

What's that? [*calls*] What?

THE DOOR OPENS. **MALCOLM** LOOKS IN.

MALCOLM

Your auntie was wondering...[*registers Ethan*] Hell's teeth! Your face!

ETHAN

I walked into a door. Didn't I?

MALCOLM

Don't tell Aunt Charlotte. She'll go mad. I'll sort you out.

SCENE 30. STREET AT FRONT OF HOUSE: EXT: DAY

TIMMS APPROACHES THE HOUSE CAUTIOUSLY. HE LOOKS AT UPPER WINDOWS AND TRIES A LOW WHISTLE BUT THERE'S NO RESPONSE.

HE RINGS THE BELL. **CHARLOTTE** OPENS THE DOOR.

CHARLOTTE

Yes?

TIMMS

Is Beth in?...Ethan?

CHARLOTTE

No.

TIMMS

Oh. Are you [*slight stutter*] sure?

CHARLOTTE

Are you calling me a liar?

TIMMS

Er, no.

CHARLOTTE

See the notice? No callers of any kind.

TIMMS

Oh yes. Then - w-what's the bell for?

CHARLOTTE

I beg your pardon??

                         TIMMS
Do you know where they are? I've got my bike.

                         CHARLOTTE
No I do not.

                         TIMMS
I've got this map for them.

                         CHARLOTTE
Map? What Map?

                         TIMMS
[*showing the map*] This.

                         CHARLOTTE
Give it here. [*takes the map*] Now buzz off.

                         TIMMS
I...oh.

SHE GOES IN AND SLAMS DOOR.

                         TIMMS
[*Terminator impression*] I'll be back.

SCENE 31. HOME. OFFICE: INT: DAY

A SMALL ROOM WITH A LARGE ROLL TOP DESK. **CHARLOTTE** ENTERS. SHE CHECKS NO ONE IS CLOSE THEN MAKES A DECISIVE MOVEMENT THAT WE CAN'T QUITE SEE CLEARLY. THE SECRET DRAWER OPENS WITH A CLUNK. WE CAN'T SEE WHAT'S IN THE DRAWER. IT IS OF GENEROUS PROPORTIONS. SHE PLACES THE MAP IN THE DRAWER AND CLOSES IT, CHECKING THAT IT'S SECURELY CLOSED. SHE HEARS A FAINT THUD ON THE DOOR.

                         CHARLOTTE
Who's that? Who's there?

SHE OPENS THE DOOR. **MALCOLM** IS NOT QUITE CAUGHT SPYING.

                         CHARLOTTE
You spying on me?

MALCOLM

Why? What's going on?

CHARLOTTE

Why am I feeding you, Malcolm?

MALCOLM

Well, it's just while I'm between jobs, dear...in a sort of space.

CHARLOTTE

You are a sort of space. A waste of skin.

MALCOLM

Yes, dear.

SCENE 32. OUTSIDE TIMMS' FLAT: EXT: DAY

IN A ROUGH UNCULTIVATED AREA BEHIND SOME FLATS WHERE THERE IS THE INEVITABLE SUPERMARKET TROLLEY AND A MOULDY STAIR CARPET, WE APPROACH A DILAPIDATED TREE HOUSE. VOICE OF **TIMMS** CAN BE HEARD.

SCENE 33. TREE HOUSE: EXT: DAY

THERE IS ONE GARDEN CHAIR AND SOME ANTIQUE CUSHIONS TO SIT ON. BY THE CLOTHES THE **KIDS** ARE WEARING THIS MUST BE THE END OF THE SCHOOL DAY. THERE IS A LADDER LEADING INTO THE TREE HOUSE.

TIMMS

Well. Let's s-sum up what we've got.

BETH

I'm cold.

ETHAN

So are we.

BETH

I mean we've not got nothing. Why are we looking for this Russian girl? I want to look for Mum.

ETHAN

Go home if you want to.

TIMMS

Oh, come on you two! We've got Zara's message. She says here... 'Sometimes in the morning, I can feel the sun shining in through the little porthole.' Right. The sun rises in the east, yeah?

ETHAN

Yeah!

TIMMS

So the boat most likely must be moored facing north or south so that bit of the river runs north south. That helps.

ETHAN

[*delighted*] That is wicked!

BETH

There's lots of north south bits of the Thames.

ETHAN

Whose side are you on?

TIMMS

No! Wait! Look at her list. She can't see anything but she mentions all the things she can hear. Water birds and owls.

ETHAN

Not much help.

TIMMS

No but a distant big road and 'fireworks.' She can smell fireworks!

BETH

You get fireworks all over.

ETHAN

She can hear church bells! See?

TIMMS

That's useful.

BETH

There's lots of churches.

ETHAN

Trains!

TIMMS

If we could put bells and trains and roads together.

ETHAN

Gotta be a big town.

BETH

Mrs Farleigh's map had Reading, Windsor, Oxford...Could be anywhere.

ETHAN

She says the ducks and the trains reminded her of holidays in Bulgaria.

BETH

What of it?

TIMMS

We don't know. Not yet.

ETHAN

I'm hungry.

TIMMS

Next time I'll bring loads to eat.

ETHAN

Yeah! High five!

ALL

High five!

ETHAN

Yee ha!

HE FALLS OFF THE LADDER AND MIMES WRITHING IN AGONY.

BETH

I told Mum I wanted a sister. Look what I got.

SCENE 34. HOME OFFICE: INT: EVENING

THE **PARROT** IS ON TOP OF THE BOOKCASE NEXT TO THE DESK. ALSO ON THE BOOKCASE THERE IS AN IMPRESSIVE BUST OF QUEEN VICTORIA. **MALCOLM** HURRIES IN AND SHOUTS AT THE **PARROT**.

MALCOLM

Come down from there!

CHARLOTTE

[*looking in*] It won't listen to you. Knock it down with the broom.

MALCOLM

Yes, dear.

AS HE LEAVES THE KIDS COME IN. THE **PARROT** SQUAWKS. THEY SEE THE **PARROT** AND LAUGH.

CHARLOTTE

It's not funny!

DON BRADMAN

Liar!

BETH

Is it tea time?

CHARLOTTE

Tea time?? You come with me, young lady.

SHE HUSTLES BETH OUT OF THE ROOM AS MALCOLM RETURNS WITH THE BROOM.

ETHAN

What's up with her?

MALCOLM

Well, you are late for tea.

ETHAN

Mum wouldn't mind.

MALCOLM

Your mum's not here. Now, get up on the chair and poke him off there. He's in disgrace.

                            ETHAN

He's only a parrot.

                         DON BRADMAN

Only a parrot!

                            MALCOLM

Come on. Let's do what she says.

HELPS **ETHAN** ONTO THE CHAIR.

                            ETHAN

Don't want to hurt him.

HE INADVERTENTLY KNOCKS THE BUST DOWN ONTO THE DESK WITH A BANG. THE
SECRET DRAWER FLIES OPEN. HE JUMPS DOWN

                            ETHAN

Sorry! Oh. What's that?...There's letters!

                            MALCOLM

I didn't put them there. It's nothing to do with me.

                         DON BRADMAN

Liar!

                            MALCOLM

I'm not lying. I've never seen that drawer open. She wouldn't let me
see it. Oh God, I'm arguing with the parrot!

                            ETHAN

 They're all addressed to...us...to Beth and me...It's...they're all
 from Mum!

ETHAN GATHERS UP ALL THE LETTERS.

                            MALCOLM

You leave them alone. She'll go mad!

                            ETHAN

They're not yours. They're mine, Mine and Beth's...And that's Timmsy's
map!

                            MALCOLM

That's stealing!

DON BRADMAN

Liar!

ETHAN

Yeah! Liar!

ETHAN GOES OUT WITH THE LETTERS AND MAP. **MALCOLM** HASTILY CLOSES THE
SECRET DRAWER.

CHARLOTTE:

[Oov] Malcolm!

MALCOLM

Coming, dear.

SCENE 35.LIVING ROOM: INT: EARLY EVENING

MALCOLM ENTERS, HOPEFULLY SMILING.

CHARLOTTE

I've sent that girl to her room. Do you know what she called me?

MALCOLM

A silly old cow, was it?

CHARLOTTE

No it was not.

MALCOLM

Oh, was it a wizened old witch?

CHARLOTTE

Malcolm. Shut up! Those kids are rude and ungrateful. I've had enough.
I've done my best. They're going into care.

MALCOLM

But you promised Rowena -

CHARLOTTE

My sister's in Cloud Cuckoo Land...And there's no return ticket from
there. These kids are not down to me. I'm sorry but they're going.
I'll call the office tomorrow.

MALCOLM

Are you sure, dear??

CHARLOTTE

Don't push it!

MALCOLM

Yes, dear. No dear.

SCENE 36. KIDS' BEDROOM: AFTER MIDNIGHT: INT: NIGHT

THERE ARE OPENED LETTERS EVERYWHERE. **BETH** IS HALF LAUGHING, HALF CRYING. **ETHAN** IS CALMER.

ETHAN

Shut up crying all the time.

BETH

She loves us. She does! She never forgot us at all. Cruella hid everything. Why did she do that?

ETHAN

Grown-ups are childish.

BETH

Five kisses on this one! And she did get my postcards!

ETHAN

This is from Nick Savage. He says Mum's much better!

BETH

Yeah - much! Maybe we won't go to Rio just yet.

ETHAN

Mum could find that Russian girl!

BETH

Forget that message in a bottle thingy. It's all a con. Bit of fun. There isn't any Russian girl!

ETHAN

You what? I thought you were on my side! You said...It was all lies! The parrot would know! He can smell lies a mile off!

BETH

You're little. You don't know about things. I'll soon be getting all those growing up things...Periods and that.

ETHAN

What? Free periods for revision?

BETH

You loopy muppet! Don't they do sex in your form?

ETHAN

We did that in Year 5.

BETH

Point is, if Mum's coming back we'll need to be here. To look after her like before. We can't be followin' no wild geese up the river.

ETHAN

How d'you know she's coming back?

BETH

Cos I've read all her letters, that's why. You haven't.

ETHAN

I will.

BETH

You'll be watchin' the pigs' fly past. Gawd it's one-thirty in the morning and we've got school!

ETHAN

Yeah...Better get these out of sight. She'll do her nut!

BETH

No, she won't! She can't! They're ours and she hid them. She'll have to keep quiet.

ETHAN

She'd better an all!

BETH

Oh no! It's PE after break and I have to wash my knicks.

ETHAN

Just cry on em. That'll do it. [*he yawns mightily*]

SCENE 37. MRS PATEL'S ECONOMICS CLASS: INT: DAY

KIDS ARE TORPID.

MRS PATEL

Remember, we're in Europe. We're not in the Eurozone. You go on the bus, you pay in sterling.

ETHAN HAS HIS ARMS ON THE TABLE AND HIS HEAD ON HIS ARMS. MRS **PATEL** SPOTS THIS AND APPROACHES HIM.

MRS PATEL

What is sterling, Ethan?

SHE PRODS HIM WITH A RULER. HE WAKES UP SUDDENLY, WONDERING WHERE HE IS.

MRS PATEL

What did I say?

ETHAN

Er you said 'What did I say?'

OTHER KIDS LAUGH.

MRS PATEL

Two detentions for you, Ethan. And don't tell me you've got a paper round because I do not care. You will write me a summary of European transport. Emma, which two countries in Europe still have steam trains?

EMMA

Poland, miss.

MRS PATEL

And?

BOY

Trumpton?

GIGGLE ROUND CLASS.

MRS PATEL

All right. Not bad. But it's Bulgaria, isn't it, Ethan?

ETHAN

Yes, Miss...What?...Bulgaria?? No...Hang about!

MRS PATEL

Now what's the matter?

ETHAN

The trains! She said they reminded her of her holidays in Bulgaria! They must have been <u>steam</u> trains! Now we know where she is! She's next to a steam railway! With steam engines and steam trains! Sorted!!

HE JUMPS UP AND KISSES MRS **PATEL**.

MRS PATEL

Any more of this behaviour, you go straight to the Headmaster. Understand?

ETHAN

Yeah, yeah. It don't matter. It was all real, don't you see? Not a con. That message in the bottle was real and I'm going to find Zara!

SARCASTIC CHEER FROM THE **BOYS**.

SCENE 38. CHARLOTTE'S DINING ROOM: INT: EARLY EVENING

IT IS PAST SIX. CHARLOTTE GLARES AT MALCOLM OVER THE CHILDREN'S TEA WHICH THIS TIME IS MUCH BETTER AND FEATURES A CHOCOLATE CAKE.

CHARLOTTE

Where are they?

MALCOLM

How should I know?

CHARLOTTE

Where are those letters?

MALCOLM

I don't know. They hid them.

CHARLOTTE

How dare they!

MALCOLM

Well, you did, dear.

CHARLOTTE

Yes. For their own good. My sister is on drugs. Better for those kids if she was never heard of again.

MALCOLM

If you say so, dear. But I like the kids. Someone to talk to.

CHARLOTTE

Oh yes! You have to be on their side, don't you?

MALCOLM

They're just kids. Unhappy...

CHARLOTTE

Who isn't. I called the Council. They don't want Rowena's children. They say that I am the best person to look after them in the circumstances.

MALCOLM

That's right. You are, dear. If they go into care they'd be split up.

CHARLOTTE

Better that way. Look. A delicious chocolate cake! Untouched! Am I mean with them? Am I?

MALCOLM

No, dear. Not at all. They should be grateful. It does look delicious ...Shall we have a slice each?

CHARLOTTE

We shall not! It's going in the bin. If they want nothing at all from me, that's what they'll get.

MALCOLM

I do think, dear, that sometimes you're a bit OTT.

CHARLOTTE

A bit what?

MALCOLM

A bit too much. I mean - It's very good of you to look after those two but you know, they're just normal kids. They can't help what's happened to Rowena.

CHARLOTTE

Go and find those children and bring them back.

MALCOLM

I don't know where they are.

CHARLOTTE

Find them, or no pocket money for you.

MALCOLM REACTS.

DON BRADMAN

[*Oov*] Same as usual!

SCENE 39. TIMMS' TREE HOUSE: EXT: DAY

THE MAP OF THE THAMES IS PINNED UP ROUGHLY AND THERE IS A RED CIRCLE AROUND WALLINGFORD. AN ANCIENT CD PLAYER IS PLAYING POP MUSIC. **TIMMS, BETH** AND **ETHAN** HAVE CANS OF BEER WHICH THEY'RE DRINKING FROM THE CAN. **TIMMS**, LOOKING VERY PLEASED WITH LIFE, IS HANDING OUT THE PIZZAS IN THEIR BOXES. **TIMMS** HAS HIS HARMONICA IN HIS POCKET.

TIMMS

Americano for you, Beth. That's a hot one.

BETH

Yah! Love it!

TIMMS

The Hawaiian - That's for me.

ETHAN

Wha's that then?

                              TIMMS

Pineapple, innit? And for you, Ethan, as requested, the Mexican Hot,
15 inch diameter...You'll never finish that...

                              ETHAN

Wanna bet? Yeahhhhh!

                              BETH

Where'd you get the wonga, Timmsy?

                              TIMMS

Borrowed it from my nan.

                              BETH

Does she know?

                              TIMMS

I'm going to tell her. I will.

                              BETH

Yeah, Okay...

                              TIMMS

Listen up, you guys. Here's the deal. Once you gave me back the map I
got down to it. Now there's only one place on the Thames where you're
moored north south and you can hear a steam train and that's here just
south of Wallingford. It's a little old fashioned fun railway and only
runs some days but it's only about three-quarters of a mile from the
river. She could easily hear it on a still day.

                              ETHAN

We're going. We're going there.

                              BETH

Wait. Are we sure about this?

                              ETHAN

I'm going.

                              TIMMS

I could help out maybe.

                              BETH

No. You'll be getting into trouble just for us.

                    ETHAN

Timms could come if he wants.

                    BETH

He's done enough for us. If we do this we gotta do it on our own.

                    ETHAN

What's that? Listen.

                    TIMMS

Someone coming up the tree. I'll tell em to piss off.

MALCOLM APPEARS AT THE ENTRANCE.

                    MALCOLM

I've searched for you all over.

                    ETHAN

What are you doing here?

                    TIMMS

Fancy a drink?

                    MALCOLM

You kids are drinking beer?...Well, I am a bit thirsty. Been all over like I said.

                    BETH

Malcolm, if we come back with you, could you lend us two coach fares to Wallingford?

                    MALCOLM

You got a hell of a cheek!

                    ETHAN

Have a bit of my pizza?

TIMMS SOUNDS HIS HARMONICA TRIUMPHANTLY.

SCENE 40. STREET SCENE: EXT: DAY

MALCOLM, A MASS OF NERVES, STANDING OUTSIDE A COACH.

                    MALCOLM

[*shouting*] Be very careful!

WE SEE **BETH** AND **ETHAN** IN COACH WITH THEIR RUCKSACKS. THEY CAN'T HEAR **MALCOLM**. THEY MIME 'What??'

MALCOLM

I said be very careful!

THE COACH MOVES OFF. AS IT MOVES AWAY FROM US WE HEAR **BETH**.

BETH (VOICE OVER)

Dear Mum, We're going away for a couple of days. It's a sort of adventure. But don't worry. Well, you don't have to worry cos by the time you get this we'll be back with Auntie Charlotte. Love you lots and lots, Your Beth... Ethan sends his, too. PS. We're not exactly escaping so don't blame Aunt Charlotte. It's nothing to do with her.

SCENE 41. DINING ROOM: INT: EARLY EVENING

FIVE O'CLOCK. THE FRONT ROOM. THE TABLE HAS THE RED TEAPOT AND FOUR CUPS ON IT BUT NOTHING ELSE. **CHARLOTTE** SITS AT END OF TABLE AS IF MADE OF STONE. HER ARMS ARE CROSSED. THERE'S NO SIGN OF WEAKNESS. THE FRONT DOOR IS HEARD AND **MALCOLM** ENTERS LOOKING GUILTY.

CHARLOTTE

Well?

MALCOLM

Oh, yes, thank you, dear.

CHARLOTTE

Where have you been?

MALCOLM

Oh. here and there, dear.

CHARLOTTE

Did you steal that money?

MALCOLM

Not steal no. I did borrow some. It's all in my notebook – here.

CHARLOTTE

Where are the children?

MALCOLM

I can't tell you that.

CHARLOTTE

What? <u>What</u>?? Why not?

MALCOLM

They asked me not to.

CHARLOTTE

Are you defying me?...I said are you defying me?

MALCOLM

[*pause*] Well, yes, I suppose it must be that. I am...It's not against you, dear. I'm always on your side.

CHARLOTTE

Where are they?

MALCOLM

Don't worry. They've got return tickets.

CHARLOTTE

Where are they?

MALCOLM

Sorry, dear. They er didn't want you to be cross. They're not running away or anything.

CHARLOTTE

You - You <u>are</u> defying me.

MALCOLM

[*gently*] Well, there's a first time for everything, dear.

CHARLOTTE PICKS UP THE FULL TEAPOT AND HURLS IT AT **MALCOLM**. IT MISSES BUT MAKES A GREAT NOISE AND MESS.

CHARLOTTE RECOGNIZES THAT IT'S A DEFINING MOMENT IN HER LIFE. SHE COVERS HER FACE WITH HER HANDS.

MALCOLM

Tell you what, dear. Shall we have a lovely cup of tea? Oh. Well, not tea perhaps. Nice cup of coffee?

CHARLOTTE DOESN'T MOVE.

SCENE 42. WALLINGFORD. OUTSIDE THE COACH STATION

               ETHAN

Where are we? Where's the river?

               BETH

We crossed it, didn't we? Hold this. [*opening up the map*]

           PASSING WOMAN

Mind what you're doing, child!

               BETH

Sorry, Miss. [*as woman goes*] Child?? Sarky old cow!...Here. That's it there. That bridge.

               ETHAN

And here's the railway. Come on. How do we get there?

               BETH

Taxi would be nice. How's our money?

               ETHAN

What money?

               BETH

Never mind. It's a cool place. We'll take a taxi.

               ETHAN

You're kidding!

               BETH

No. It is cool. I lied about the taxi.

               ETHAN

I don't mind walking. It's a great evening. Fancy half a Mars bar?

               BETH

Yeahh!

               ETHAN

Yeah, wicked evening. I lied about the Mars bar.

SHE CHASES HIM DOWN THE STREET.

SCENE 43. VIEW OF THAMES AT WALLINGFORD. EVENING

NEWSREADER (VOICE OVER)

A Russian billionaire is believed to be offering a substantial reward for the return of his daughter Zara who is believed to have been kidnapped and is being held somewhere in this country. And now back to our sports coverage.

SCENE 44. THE DINING ROOM. INT: EVENING

MALCOLM IS SCRUBBING THE TEA-STAINED CARPET. ENTER **CHARLOTTE** WITH A TRAY AND TWO CUPS.

CHARLOTTE

You can stop scrubbing now. I've made you a cup of coffee.

MALCOLM

What? For me?

SCENE 45. THE BRIDGE NEAR WALLINGFORD: EXT: DAY

BETH AND **ETHAN** ARE STANDING AT THE EAST SIDE OF THE BRIDGE LOOKING AT THE RIVER.

BETH

Where's this boat then? Where's any sodding boat? Where's this flippin' Russian Princess and all that?

ETHAN

Maybe they move about. This is the place. Timms said.

BETH

Maybe Timms got it wrong. Maybe the whole caboodle never existed. Who'd send a message in a bottle these days? Eeeth! There's a London coach at half-eight.

ETHAN

Go back to ol' Cruella then. Tell her I'm not giving up.

BETH

Leave you here? Mum'd kill me. You know that. Right. Where now then? There's nothing there on the other side. Just grass. On this side there's a lane. And a big building.

ETHAN

Yeah! Hotel!

BETH

Don't be daft. Anyway, looks a bit empty if you ask me. Oh, come on then.

ETHAN

Be dark soon. We have to spend the night somewhere.

BETH

If Mum was here, it'd all be fun. An adventure.

ETHAN

Well, it is. Innit?

BETH

It's all a con, Eeth. a sort of joke. And we fell for it. There's nothing here. Oh. That looks like a churchyard.

ETHAN

Don't like churchyards.

SCENE 46. DINING ROOM: INT: NIGHT

MALCOLM AND CHARLOTTE ARE HAVING A CUP OF COFFEE. CHARLOTTE IS LOOKING TEARFUL.

MALCOLM

What's the matter, love?

AT LAST SHE BURSTS INTO TEARS. MALCOLM VAGUELY WANTS TO COMFORT HER BUT FAILS.

MALCOLM

Oh, love!

CHARLOTTE

When are they coming back, Malcolm? The kids?

MALCOLM

Soon, dear. Soon.

CHARLOTTE

When they're not here it's so bloody...quiet...

SCENE 47. OUTSIDE CHURCH DOOR: EXT: NIGHT

BETH

[*increasingly miserable*] All locked. That building's locked an all. We've just made friggin' fools of ourselves. You have anyway.

ETHAN

But we can see all along the river from here. Or we would if it wasn't dark.

BETH

Nasty old night eh? Decided to get dark just to make you look silly. Shit! What would Mum do?

ETHAN

[*close to tears*] She's not here. She's not here, Beth.

BETH

She'd say let's be sensible. Cut our losses. Time to go home and that's where I'm going.

ETHAN

We've missed the coach now.

BETH

I don't care. You can either come with me or not. [*pause*] 'Bye then. Have a nice time.

SHE WALKS AWAY.

ETHAN

[*calling out*] That message was for me! I'm not backing down!

BETH

[*quietly*] Oh, get lost.

SCENE 48. DINING ROOM: INT: NIGHT

CHARLOTTE HAS THAT CUP OF COFFEE IN FRONT OF HER. **MALCOLM** LOOKS MORE RELAXED.

> **MALCOLM**
>
> I promised them and I can't go back on my word.

> **CHARLOTTE**
>
> Where are they? You've got to tell me. Never mind your bloody world. What am I going to tell my sister?

SCENE 49. OPEN LAND WITH PATH RUNNING THROUGH: EXT: NIGHT

BETH IS WALKING PAST THE FACTORY PLACE. NO LIGHTS ARE ON.

> **BETH (VOICE OVER)**
>
> Why did I ever listen to him - or that idiot, Timms? I'll never open a bottle again! I have to carry everything.

SHE SLOWS DOWN.

> **BETH**
>
> Oh no! I've got all the food haven't I?

SHE STOPS AND CHECKS HER RUCKSACK.

> **BETH**
>
> He's going to starve. His fault...What a sodding life! Oh...bugger! The silly dork has got to eat!

SHE SHRUGS, THEN TURNS AND VERY SLOWLY WALKS BACK TOWARDS THE CHURCH. SOMEONE IS APPROACHING AT A HALF RUN.

> **BETH**
>
> [out loud] Who's that? Who is it?

> **ETHAN**
>
> Thought you'd gone.

> **BETH**
>
> What do you want?

> **ETHAN**

Nothing.

> **BETH**

Forgot about the food, didn't you? Big brave traveller! Dr Livingstone, I assume.

> **ETHAN**

All right. I'm hungry. It's not against the law.

> **BETH**

[*moving towards the church with more determination*] The churchyard then. I saw this grave with a flat top. We can put the food out on there.

> **ETHAN**

Yeah! Picnic!

> **BETH**

I have to think of everything.

> **ETHAN**

I got a torch. It works a bit.

> **BETH**

All right. One up to you.

THEY HURRY ON TOWARDS THE CHURCH.

SCENE 50. A ROADSIDE: EXT: NIGHT

A **BOY** WALKS TOWARD THE WEST, CHEERFULLY PLAYING HIS HARMONICA AND THUMBING A LIFT. CARS PASS BUT ONE STOPS. HE RUNS TOWARDS CAR BUT IT'S A POLICE CAR.

> **POLICEMAN**

Going somewhere, sir?

> **TIMMS**

Maybe.

> **POLICEMAN**

How old are you, son?

TIMMS

S...seventeen.

POLICEMAN

Like seventeen going on - fourteen?

TIMMS

It's fifteen.

POLICEMAN

We might have to hold you for questioning.

TIMMS

Why? What have I done?

POLICEMAN

It's the only way we can give you a lift. Hop in.

TIMMS

I do s-support the Police.

POLICEMAN

I knew there was one.

TIMMS GETS IN THE CAR.

SCENE 51. GRAVEYARD: EXT: NIGHT

BETH AND **ETHAN** ARE SITTING EITHER SIDE OF A GRAVE. THE TORCH GVES A LAST WEAK LIGHT.

BETH

That torch of yours...Typical! I think you just ate a snail.

ETHAN

No, I didn't 't. Look. [*shines the last weak light on the inscription*] Look. 'Agatha Gwent. Sadly missed by all who knew her.'

BETH

She's done us a favour an' all. Ta, Aggie!

ETHAN

In the morning we can see up and down the river.

> BETH

And if there's nothing we go back.

> ETHAN

Back to Cruella and marge?

> BETH

Who's Marge?

> ETHAN

It's what she puts on the bread, innit.

> BETH

Ho ho! Now, are you scared to spend the night here?

> ETHAN

Not if you're not.

> BETH

I quite liked that one over there. It's like a little house. We can't get in it but there's a sort of porch. We can try and sleep there.

> ETHAN

It's cold.

> BETH

It's just one night. If there's ghosts we'll run back to the road. If you hear a scream in the night, that'll be foxes. Like on radio. It's not banshees and that.

> ETHAN

Vampires live in graveyards.

> BETH

What do you know? They aren't allowed on holy ground. If a vampire does turn up you make the sign of a cross like that.

> ETHAN

And then what?

> BETH

Run like hell.

AN OWL HOOTS.

SCENE 52. STREET: EXT: NIGHT

THE POLICE CAR HAS STOPPED. **TIMMS** GETS OUT.

> **TIMMS**
>
> Ta. I can walk from here.

> **POLICEMAN**
>
> Does your mum know you're out?

> **TIMMS**
>
> She don't care. She went off with a bloke from Watford.

> **POLICEMAN**
>
> Happens to the best of us.

> **TIMMS**
>
> I left a note for my nan. If she can find her glasses.

> **POLICEMAN**
>
> Watch out for yourself then.

> **TIMMS**
>
> Bin doing that for seven years.

> **POLICEMAN**
>
> 'Night then.

> **TIMMS**
>
> See ya later.

THE **POLICE** WAVE AND DRIVE AWAY.

SCENE 53. GRAVEYARD: EXT: EARLY MORNING

BETH WAKES UP AFTER A TERRIBLE NIGHT TO FIND HERSELF ALONE. SHE SEES **ETHAN** STANDING AT THE EDGE OF THE GRAVEYARD, LOOKING OUT ACROSS THE RIVER.

> **ETHAN**
>
> All right then. Is that a boat or is that a boat?

> **BETH**
>
> Bloody hell! Jammy bugger...'Course, we don't know what boat it is.

                              ETHAN

No one's come and gone. I know it's them.

                              BETH

Right. We cross the bridge and walk along the towpath, all innocent-
like and see what's what...

                              ETHAN

If we get caught they could tie us up and we'd be sending messages
in bottles.

                              BETH

Who'd pay a ransom for you?

                              ETHAN

Mum would.

                              BETH

If we go on board that boat that's trespassing. It's against the law.
Everything's against people like us.

                              ETHAN

What we got to lose then?

                              BETH

Race you to the bridge!

SHE STARTS RUNNING.

                              ETHAN

That's not fair...

HE FOLLOWS.

SCENE 54. THE OTHER SIDE OF THE RIVER: EXT: DAY

THEY COME OUT OF THE BUSHES AT THE END OF THE TWISTING PATH AND THEY ARE
ON FLAT GROUND WITH NO COVER.

                              BETH

[Sotto] Look normal. Like we're going for a walk.

ETHAN STARTS TO HUM IN A CASUAL WAY.

BETH

And don't make that noise.

ETHAN

I was singing.

BETH

You coulda fooled me.

THEY WALK PAST THE BOAT WHICH LOOKS NORMAL. THEY STOP.

BETH

I don't think there's anyone on board.

ETHAN

I've got it all planned. We walk past and very quietly we call out 'Zara!' We know she can hear things.

BETH

No, you noodle! They'll get suspicious. Let's go aboard all innocent like and say we're lost.

ETHAN

[*Whispering*] Oh yes. All right.

BETH

No need to whisper. We're lost, right? [*aloud*] I think we're lost, Charlie.

ETHAN

[*Sotto*] Who's Charlie?

BETH

[*Sotto*] We don't tell em our real names, do we?

ETHAN

Oh yeah. [*aloud and badly acted*] Let's try the people on this boat, Celia!

BETH

[*Sotto*] Celia??? [*aloud*] Okay, Charlie. Give us a hand.

SHE GETS ONTO THE BOAT AND LISTENS. NOTHING. SHE HELPS **'CHARLIE'** ONTO THE BOAT.

                         BETH

Hello? Anyone at home?

                         ETHAN

Er ahoy there! Anyone on board?

SILENCE. A PASSING DUCK MAKES THEM JUMP. **BETH** TAPS ON THE DOUBLE DOOR
THAT LEADS BELOW

                         BETH

  Hello?...I can hear something.

                         ETHAN

Open it then.

                         BETH

  I'm going to...

SHE OPENS THE DOORS A FINGER'S WIDTH APART AND SUDDENLY A LARGE DOG HURLS
HIMSELF AGAINST THE OPENING, SNARLING AND GROWLING IN A WAY THAT LEAVES
NO DOUBT ABOUT HIS INTENTIONS. BETH AND ETHAN RUN AWAY FOR SOME FIFTY
METRES AND STOP, REALIZING THE DOG IS NOT PURSUING. THEY ARE GASPING
WITH FEAR.

                         BETH

  Better think again, eh?

                         ETHAN

Don't like big dogs.

                         BETH

Someone coming!

                         ETHAN

We can hide in the bushes. I want a pee anyway.

                         BETH

Me too. That was scary...Why don't we go home, Eeth? Hang on! Look!
In't that...?

                         ETHAN

It's Timmsy! Hey, Tim! [recovering his swagger]
What you doin' here, ol' mate?

TIMMS

I...d-didn't want to miss the fun...

ETHAN

Right! We spent the night in a graveyard. As you do.

TIMMS

I was in a bus shelter.

ETHAN

Nice one...Got any grub?

TIMMS

Did have but I ate it. Is that the boat?

BETH

Yeah but there's a socking great dog.

TIMMS

Thought there might be. Right. Got any money?

BETH AND ETHAN

No.

TIMMS

Mm. Can you sing?

BETH

Never tried.

TIMMS

Time to start then.

SCENE 55. THE FINSBURY PARK HOUSE AT THE FRONT DOOR: EXT: DAY

NICK SAVAGE IS TALKING TO MALCOLM WHO IS LOOKING PERKIER AND SMARMIER THAN BEFORE.

MALCOLM

My wife is none too well at the present time, Mr Savage. I'm in charge of things here.

NICK

It's the children I'm hoping to see. Their mother sent me.

MALCOLM

Of course. As it happens they are away at the moment.

NICK

[*Worried*] Away? Where?

MALCOLM

Well, I could help you there. Direct you. I could even come with you. But I am of course a busy man so my expenses would be an issue. I'm sure we can deal with that. Shall we chat over some nice coffee and biscuits...?

SCENE 56. A QUIET STREET: EXT: DAY

TIMMS IS PLAYING 'LARA'S THEME' ON HIS HARMONICA AS **BETH** TRILLS ALONG. SHE HAS A GOOD VOICE SO THE COMBINED EFFECT IS QUITE MUSICAL. **ETHAN** APPROACHES PEDESTRIAN WITH A SMALL PLASTIC BAG CONTAINING SOME COINS.

ETHAN

Oh. Hello. We're collecting for imprisoned Russian children.

WOMAN

Never heard of it. And you should be in school.

ETHAN

We've got special permission. It's er Mr Putin's Birthday!

WOMAN

Nonsense! Oh...She's got a nice voice. Here. [*gives him 10p*]

ETHAN

Oh, ta!

TIMMS

[*stopping his playing*] I think we've got enough for the food.

ETHAN

I'm really hungry.

BETH

It's not for you! It's for the dog.

THEY HURRY AWAY AS **TIMMS** TRIES TO COUNT THE MONEY.

SCENE 57. NICK SAVAGE'S CAR: INT: DAY

NICK

Where's this?

MALCOLM

This is Nettlebed. Nearly there. I must say I'm enjoying this. I don't get out so much. The wife has the car. Very much so.

NICK

Yes...You're sure you know where the children have gone?

MALCOLM

Mr Savage, do I look like a liar?

SCENE 58. THE WEST SIDE OF THE RIVER: EXT: DAY

IN MIDSHOT THE BOAT AS BEFORE. TWO CYCLISTS PASS ON THE TOWPATH BUT OTHERWISE IT'S QUIET BUT FOR DISTANT BIRDSONG.

PAN ACROSS TO THE BUSHES BY THE WINDING PATH ON THE WEST SIDE OF THE BRIDGE. IN A SHELTERED CORNER, **TIMMS**, **BETH** AND **ETHAN** ARE STUDYING THE MAP.

BETH

Timms! We never planned to steal a boat!

TIMMS

If Z-Zara's there it'll take a while to get her off unhurt. If we take the boat we have more time to deal with Z-Zara.

BETH

How do we start the engine?

TIMMS

We don't. The boat will drift downstream.

ETHAN

What? to London?

TIMMS

No. If we haven't found the girl, if it's the wrong boat-

BETH

Bet it is.

TIMMS

If it's the wrong boat we get to the side, the bank...

ETHAN

Then what?

TIMMS

We get out and run for it. If we find the girl and no one's after us we drift down to the weir at Streatley and take her to the police station. Bound to be one. But if the kidnap blokes are after us I'll call the cops on my mobile and we'll hope for the best.

BETH

It's...scary!

TIMMS

If the girl exists, she's your job, Beth.

ETHAN

She does exist. She's on that boat. Trust me!

TIMMS

Yeah. Now. The dog first and then we'll see how we go.

ETHAN

I'm not going near that dog!

TIMMS

Leave him to me but soon as I say, you get on the boat and cast off. If the dog swims back to the boat, push him off with something.

BETH

Timms, why can't we just call the police now and let them deal with it?

TIMMS

If it's the wrong boat we're in trouble, bunking off, wasting police time, all that. We've got to see it through.

BETH

All right then. Anyone in sight?

ETHAN

Nobody.

TIMMS

Let's go then. Good luck everybody.

ETHAN

That was in a film!

TIMMS

You bet!

THEY SET OUT.

ETHAN

[*Sotto*] Are you scared?

BETH

Dead scared. And all this was your idea. Remember that!

ETHAN

Listen! The train. It's gotta be the right place!

BETH

Was it even the right bottle?

THEY HAVE REACHED THE BOAT. THEY LISTEN.

TIMMS

Let's go!

TIMMS DUMPS A LARGE JUICY BONE ON THE TOWPATH AND TAKES A BAG OF UNCOOKED MEAT ONTO THE BOAT. THE **DOG** BARKS.

TIMMS

Hello, boy! It's teatime!

HE HOLDS A PIECE OF RAW STEAK AGAINST THE DOORS. THE DOG WHIMPERS.

ETHAN

Untie the boat!

TIMMS

Good boy...Come on then.

HE OPENS THE DOORS. THE **DOG** COMES OUT GROWLING, THEN SEES AND SMELLS THE MEAT. HE STILL GROWLS AT **TIMMS**.

> **TIMMS**
>
> Good boy! Here's another piece! Mmmm!

THE **DOG** STOPS GROWLING AND WOLFS DOWN THE MEAT. **TIMMS** HOLDS A JUICY BONE IN FRONT OF THE **DOG**. THE **DOG** SNAPS AT IT BUT **TIMMS** HOLDS IT UP OUT OF REACH AND THEN THROWS IT ONTO THE TOWPATH. THE **DOG** LEAPS OFF THE BOAT AND SEES THE BONES IN FRONT OF HIM.

> **TIMMS**
>
> Cast off! Hurry.

BETH AND **ETHAN** UNTIE THE BOAT AND AS THEY GET ABOARD **TIMMS** IS PUSHING THE BOAT AWAY FROM THE BANK.

> **TIMMS**
>
> Find something to row with.

> **ETHAN**
>
> Can't you start the engine?

> **TIMMS**
>
> Got a key, have you? Anything you can row with. Get her into the middle of the river. What's the dog doing?

> **ETHAN**
>
> He's doing a poo.

> **TIMMS**
>
> Good boy! That'll take him a while. What's down there?

> **ETHAN**
>
> [peering into the cabin] Er...Golf clubs?

> **TIMMS**
>
> Get me a heavy club. No paddles anywhere?

> **ETHAN**
>
> No paddles...

> **TIMMS**
>
> And we're up shit creek.

ETHAN

Where?...There's a sort of fish net thing.

TIMMS

That's your paddle. So paddle like crazy.

BETH

[*finding another small door*] Oh, Mum! Please...We've come such a long way...

SHE OPENS THE DOOR. THE **GIRL** IS TIED UP AND HAS ONLY AN EMPTY COKE BOTTLE AND A FULL POTTY. SHE LOOKS TERRIFIED AND CRINGES AWAY FROM **BETH**.

BETH

It's all right. I'm your friend. I'm Beth.

THE **GIRL** WEEPS AND SHAKES HER HEAD.

BETH

[*Whispers*] Keep still. I won't hurt you.

BETH CAREFULLY UNTIES THE **GIRL**'S BLINDFOLD.

BETH

Zara?...Zara? I'm going to take your blindfold off. It might be a bit sort of bright to start with...so get ready to shut your eyes. Anyway, here we go...

SHE REMOVES THE BLINDFOLD. THE **GIRL** BLINKS AND HER EYES FILL WITH TEARS.

BETH

I'll get you some water...

BETH SEES **ETHAN** STARING IN AT HER.

ETHAN

You said...Well?

BETH

All right, Clever Dick!

ETHAN

Yeaaahhh! (*he punches the air*) Ouch!

BETH BURSTS INTO TEARS.

                              TIMMS

   Get up here. Too slow! We're not going anywhere!

                              ETHAN

   Sorry...

                              BETH

   Water... [*cannot find anything*]

                              TIMMS

   What's going down?

                              ETHAN

   Girls are cryin'.

                              TIMMS

   Girls?? Yeeee ha!

THE **DOG** TURNS AND BARKS, SEES THE BOAT HALF WAY ACROSS THE RIVER AND
JUMPS IN.

                              TIMMS

   Here comes the pooch! Whack him on the nose.

THE **DOG** APPROACHES THE BOAT. **TIMMS** WHACKS HIM WITH A NUMBER SEVEN
IRON.

                              TIMMS

   It's okay. He can't reach...And he's bleeding...Last treat coming
   up.

HE WAVES A LAST PIECE OF MEAT AT THE **DOG** AND HURLS IT TOWARDS THE BANK.
THE **DOG** FOLLOWS IT.

                       ANGRY WEEKEND SAILOR

   You! You're the wrong side of the river. Get over!

                              TIMMS

   Oh. Sorry.

                       ANGRY WEEKEND SAILOR

   Are you under control?

TIMMS

Yes. I mean aye aye...Just fixing the engine. Thank you.

ANGRY WEEKEND SAILOR

Riff raff! Kids...I don't know...

CUT TO **BETH** GIVING **ZARA** A DRINK. **ZARA** STILL TEARFUL BUT FROM A POCKET IN
HER JEANS PRODUCES A KEY.

BETH

For the engine?

ZARA

[*Nodding*] Mo...tor.

ETHAN

Timms, I think that's them!

TIMMS

Could be big trouble...

THREE MEN GET OUT OF A VAN THEY HAVE DARK GLASSES AND ARE QUITE WELL
DRESSED. SUITS BUT NO TIES. ONE IS A MINDER. ONE MAN SPEAKS QUITE CALMLY
WITH A SMALL MEGAPHONE.

MAN 1

You kids! Don't mind you having fun but that boat is stolen. Bring
it to this bank now and we won't call the Police.

ETHAN

What do we do?

TIMMS

He's bluffing. He can't call the Police.

THE **MAN** WITH THE MEGAPHONE NODS TO THE MINDER WHO TAKES OFF HIS JACKET.

ETHAN

The big one's coming! Oh, sugar ...

BETH

Timms! The key! For the engine!

AS SHE HANDS IT TO HIM, SHE DROPS IT.

BETH

Oh sorry!

SHE SCRABBLES FOR THE KEY.

ETHAN

Hurry!...Girls...

BETH

It must be here!

ETHAN

He's a good swimmer!

TIMMS

Hurry up! Whack his hands!

ETHAN

He'd kill me!

BETH

[*weeping*] Here! Here it is.

THE **MINDER** GRABS HOLD OF THE BOAT. JUST THEN THE ENGINE STARTS AND THE BOAT SURGES FORWARD. HE HOLDS ON THEN LOSES HIS GRIP. HE CAN BE SEEN SHOUTING AS THE BOAT ACCELERATES AWAY.

TIMMS

Now we're cooking on gas!

ETHAN

Look out! Boat coming - Go right - No, left! Left!

TIMMS

You mean port.

THE OTHER BOAT (LARGER) SOUNDS A HORN AS IT PASSES VERY CLOSE BY, IN THE CABIN **ZARA** STILL LOOKS TERRIFIED AS BETH STARTS TO UNTIE HER. BETH TOO IS QUITE TEARFUL.

BETH

We'll be all right. Just a little boat trip and...Oh, I wish you spoke English! We could be friends.

                              TIMMS

Ethan, take over the wheel.

                              ETHAN

Me?

                              TIMMS

There's no one else here.

                              ETHAN

I don't know how...

                              TIMMS

I'm going to call the police, Keep her straight...Straight!

                              ETHAN

Is it like a car? I can do cars.

                              TIMMS

Starboard a tad!

                              ETHAN

What?

TIMMS GETS HIS MOBILE OUT OF HIS POCKET AND TAKES NO FURTHER INTEREST IN
THE STEERING.

                              ETHAN

I could be great at this...Oh yes!...[*looks behind*] Boat coming up
behind us, fast!

                    WOMAN ON BOAT COMING UPSTREAM

What are you doing? Look out!!

THEY SCRAPE AGAINST THE BOAT AS IT PASSES.

                              TIMMS

Push the throttle forward.

                              ETHAN

Throttle? Which is it?

                              TIMMS

That one!

BETH IS WASHING ZARA'S FACE WITH A DAMP TEA TOWEL. SHE HOLDS UP A MIRROR FOR ZARA. THIS WASN'T A GOOD IDEA. ZARA STARTS WEEPING ALL OVER AGAIN.

BETH

You'll be okay, Zara. I'd lend you some make-up but Auntie won't let me have any.

TIMMS

[*on phone*] We didn't steal the boat. We only borrowed it to rescue the girl. We fed the dog, right? We're going down to the weir at Streatley. Can you meet us there?...No! This is not a joke. They are chasing us. We rescued the girl...What do you mean 'Fairy Story'-? I'm not making this up! All right. If 100 can't help, I'll try 999

ETHAN

They're too fast for us! Timmsy!

TIMMS

Top speed! We gotta get there before they catch us!

ETHAN

I can't go any faster.

TIMMS

Look out!

ANOTHER BOAT HOOTS AT THEM AND PASSES.

RIVER POLICE

River police! Stop your engine!

ETHAN:

It's the filth! The good guys!

TIMMS:

So they say. All right. Stop.

ETHAN

Where's the brakes?

TIMMS

Switch off.

ETHAN

Oh yeah.

THE ENGINE STOPS.

BETH

What's happening?

ETHAN

Timms! You were calling the fuzz. Here they are!

TIMMS

Not this lot, I wasn't.

RIVER POLICEMAN

[*as police launch draws alongside*] This cabin cruiser is reported stolen. You...You're just kids!

TIMMS

No we're not. Bring the girl, Beth.

RIVER POLICEMAN

You were fooling about. You saw this boat and you just happened to take it?

ETHAN

No! We're the goodies, don't you see?

BETH

[*with* **ZARA**] Here she is. Zara.

RIVER POLICEMAN

More kids...Zara?...This is the girl reported missing? Possibly kidnapped! You lot are under arrest for stealing one cabin cruiser and kidnapping one child for the purposes of profit. You do not have to say anything-

TIMMS, BETH AND ETHAN

Nooooooo!

ETHAN

We rescued her! We are the good guys! We're the heroes! Get with it!

RIVER POLICEMAN

We will proceed to Streatley and you can tell your story to the Officer in Charge. And it better be good!

SCENE 59. STREET PAVEMENT: EXT: DAY

TIMMS, **BETH** AND **ETHAN** ON THE PAVEMENT AS AN AMBULANCE LEAVES. IT IS FOLLOWED BY A POLICE CAR. THE **POLICE** WAVE. THE **KIDS** WAVE BACK.

BETH

'Bye, Zara...I wish we could keep her.

TIMMS

Hope her dad wants her back.

ETHAN

He never paid the ransom, did he?

TIMMS

We could adopt her!

BETH

Wish someone could adopt us...What now?

ETHAN

I just realized! I'm so hungry! I've never in all my life been so hungry!

TIMMS

Me too. Wish I'd kept that juicy bone!

NICK SAVAGE'S CAR STOPS BY THEM. **MALCOLM** GETS OUT.

MALCOLM

Well well! Looks like we won!

ALL THREE

We?

MALCOLM

Who paid your coach fares? Moi! I have made enquiries. There could be a reward in this case. If so, I'm willing to go halves with you. How's that?

THEY STARE.

MALCOLM

Well, think it over. Oh! More good news. Your Auntie Charlotte is going to collect you personally. I'm meeting her at the coach station. You'll be home by ten o'clock.

ETHAN

What do we do now? It's all over. Everyone's gone.

MALCOLM

Oh no. My good friend Mr Savage is going to take you for a slap up dinner!

NICK

[*looking out of car*] Hello!

BETH

Nick!

NICK

Come on! Get in the car. I've booked in a hotel - Just a couple of miles.

ALL

Yeah!

THEY FORGET **MALCOLM** AND TUMBLE INTO THE CAR.

SCENE 60. COUNTRY HOTEL: INT: DAY

TYPICAL COUNTRY HOTEL, FRIENDLY RATHER THAN POSH.

NICK

Come in. Oh, before we go in the dining room, there's someone who wants to meet you.

BETH

Auntie Charlotte? Do we have to?

NICK

No, not Aunty Charlotte. Someone else. [*he whispers to* **TIMMS** *who grins*] They're through that door.

ETHAN

Oh all right then. If we must.

BETH AND **ETHAN** GO THROUGH THE DOOR.

SCENE 61. REVERSE SHOT OF CHILDREN ENTERING THE ROOM: INT: DAY

WE SEE THE **KIDS** COME THROUGH THE DOOR AND TRY TO MAKE OUT WHO IS SITTING THERE.

BETH

Eeth...It's...

BOTH

Mum!!!!

THEY RACE FORWARDS, ALL FLYING ARMS AND LEGS.

FREEZE

END.

www.ingramcontent.com/pod-product-compliance
Lightning Source LLC
Chambersburg PA
CBHW080716250626

47170CB00009B/2793